IF I WERE
A MOOSE

Written By Patrick Kleinen
Illustrated By Jeannie Winston

This edition is published and
distributed exclusively
by Discovery Toys, Inc.

Printed in Singapore for Discovery Toys
Illustrations copyright © Jeannie Winston, 1995
Text copyright © Discovery Toys, 1995

Discovery Toys, Inc. Martinez, CA 94553 U.S.A. 1-800-426-4777
Discovery Toys Canada, Inc. Burlington, Ontario L7L 6A6
Discovery Toys de México S.A. de C.V. Naucalpan, Edo. de México 53370

ISBN 0-9399790-04

Foreword

High self-esteem is based on the child's belief that he or she is lovable and competent. People with good self-esteem have a positive regard for the self, adequate confidence, are happily involved with others, feel free to take chances and learn and have pride in themselves and their accomplishments.

The heart of this story is the unconditional love that Momma has for Coopie. Throughout this story, Momma demonstrates her love in many situations. Young children will find a consistent and clear message: A parent's love for a child is never-ending — no matter what the child is like at any given moment. Raising children with unconditional love will become the foundation for their positive self-esteem and confidence.

It's never too early to talk to your children about their special qualities. Encourage them to feel proud of who they are and what they can do, because they are unique.

Following are some basic guidelines for nurturing your child's self-worth:
- Give your child the message that he or she is always lovable
- Tell your child when he or she is behaving in ways that please you or demonstrate growth
- When your child misbehaves, address the behavior, not your child's personality
- Encourage your child to share his or her feelings
- Listen attentively, in a non-judgmental manner, and with respect and acceptance
- Spend time with your child
- Give your child the respect you would any adult
- Acknowledge and respect your child's perspective
- Offer friendly guidance
- Support your child's explorations, interests, imagination and capabilities
- Have realistic expectations and expect mistakes on your child's part as well as your own

The enclosed, beautifully illustrated notepads are a wonderful way to express your feelings toward your child. They also provide a good way to reinforce positive behavior. Some notepads are designed to allow you to write any message you'd like. Others have the beginnings of a statement and leave it to you to finish with a specific message to your child. Writing something as simple as, "I love it when you...give me a kiss good-bye in the mornings" or "I love you...even when we have a hard morning" takes very little time to write, yet means so much to a child.

Place the notes in your child's lunch box, on his or her pillow or on the night stand. Your child will have a delightful surprise that conveys your personal message of encouragement, pride and unconditional love — the ingredients for self-esteem. Your child may also want to use the notepads to write or dictate a message to you.

Foreword by: The Child Development Team at Discovery Toys, Inc.

Coopie and Momma went walking to the market. It was cold outside and it took a lot of imagination to keep warm.

Coopie had plenty of imagination.

Coopie asked Momma,
"If I were a moose, do you
know what you would do?"

"I'd get myself some antlers
and a furry coat, too.
Then move into the woods...
so I could be with you!"

"If I were a kite, would you fly up high with me?"

"Oh yes!" Momma said, "And we could dance up in the clouds and soar across the sea!"

Coopie thought for awhile, then asked Momma, "If I were an angry dog and growled and barked all day...then what would you say?"

"I'd say, 'My goodness aren't you grouchy! But you just bark away! Even when you are a grouch, I love you more each day.'"

"If I were a squirrel,
do you know what you
would be?"

"If you were a squirrel,
I think I'd be a tree,
So you could sleep right
in my arms and play all
over me."

Then they snuggled on the sofa for a long time.

"Momma?"

"Yes, Coopie?"

"What if I were Coopie and nothing else but me?"

"I can't think of anything that I would rather be besides my Coopie's Momma in Coopie's family."

Then Momma gave Coopie a big hug and a kiss.

Coopie liked that.

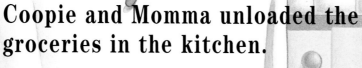

Coopie and Momma unloaded the groceries in the kitchen.

And Coopie kept on wondering.

"If I were a tummy, do you know what you would be?"

"I'd be a couple fingers and tickle you like this...see?"

Momma tickled Coopie and they both laughed and giggled.

Coopie imagined more and wondered what else there was to be...a fish, a pig, a movie star...a fence, a cow, a racing car.

"There are so many things to be," thought Coopie, "and there is only one of me!"

"If I were a parakeet, then
what would you do?"

"I think I'd be a cockatoo and
fly away with you!"

"If I were a shadow, would I b
as tall as you?"

"Maybe yes and maybe no sinc
I would be one, too!"

"If I were a rainbow, Momma, then what would you be?"

"I'd be the sun and shine on you for everyone to see."

Coopie and Momma had all their groceri[es] and started walking home.

"If I were a pigeon, would you make me fly away?"

"I'd rather be the lady who feeds you everyday."

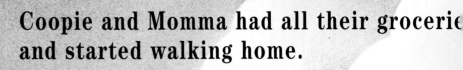

At the market, Coopie wondered about a lot of things.

"Would you chase me from the grocery store if I were a hungry dinosaur?"

"Oh no," Momma said, "I'd make sure you got enough to eat. Then we'd top it off with something sweet."

Coopie liked being a dinosaur.

EGG'S
25¢